A Special Gift

To you:

_____

From me:

_____

Today:

_____

Stories, sayings, and scriptures to Encourage and Inspire the

hugs™

for

kids

Mary Hollingsworth

HOWARD
PUBLISHING CO.

Hugs for Kids © 2000 by Mary Hollingsworth
All rights reserved. Printed in the United States of America
Published by Howard Publishing Co., Inc.,
3117 North 7th Street, West Monroe, LA 71291-2227

01 02 03 04 05 06 07 08 09   10 9 8 7 6 5 4

Interior illustrations and design by Vanessa Bearden
Edited by Philis Boultinghouse

Library of Congress Cataloging-in-Publication Data
Hollingsworth, Mary, 1947-
    Hugs for kids : stories, sayings, and scriptures to encourage and inspire / Mary
Hollingsworth.
        p. cm.
    Summary: A collection of stories and Bible verses that show how and why God
loves children.
    ISBN 1-58229-096-2
    1. Children—Religious life. 2. Chirstian life—Juvenile literature. [1. Christian
life.] I. Title.
BV4571.2 .H647 2000
242'.62—dc21   99-059685

    All Scriptures are quoted or adapted from The International Children's Bible,
New Century Version. Copyright © 1986, 1988 by Word Publishing. All rights
reserved.

Our purpose at
Howard Publishing is to:

• *Increase faith* in the hearts of
  growing Christians

• *Inspire holiness* in the lives of
  believers

• *Instill hope* in the hearts of
  struggling people everywhere

Because He's coming again!

Contents

You Are Terrific!

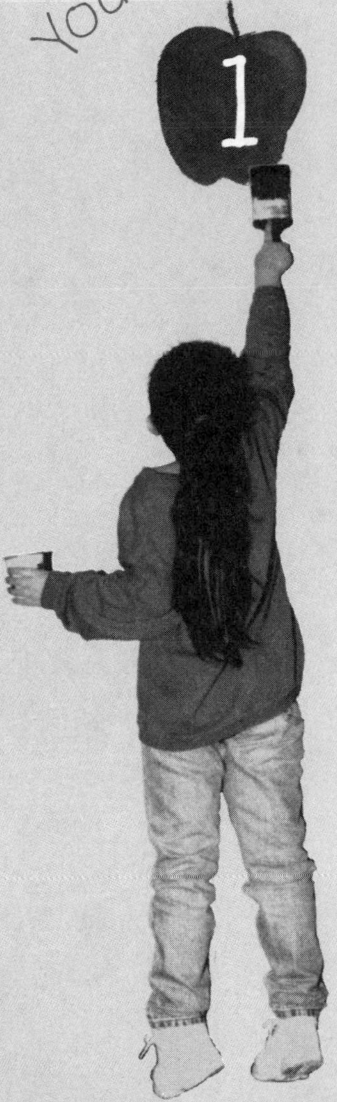

"Jesus took the children in his arms. He put his hands on them and blessed them." Mark 10:16

God Loves Children

God loves children, one and all—
Children small and children tall;
Children who have smiling faces;
Kids from all the different races.
God loves children, yessiree!
He loves you, and he loves me.

The Story of Two Bricks

One Friday night in the cold, cold winter, Mrs. Jensen went to a special meeting at the church. She took her little girl, Jenny, with her. The people were talking about how they needed a bigger church building so that more people could come and learn about Jesus. But they had a *big* problem.

They did not have enough money to build it. Everyone went home that night feeling very sad.

All that evening, Jenny sat very still and quiet looking sadly out the living room window at the snow. She hardly played with her toys at all. At last, she went to her room to bed.

The next morning, Mrs. Jensen went to Jenny's room to wake her up. She opened the door and said, "Jenny, it's time to get up."

Jenny did not answer.

"Jenny, wake up, sleepyhead. Breakfast is ready."

Jenny still did not answer.

Mrs. Jensen turned on Jenny's bedroom light. But Jenny was not there. She was gone!

Mrs. Jensen thought, *Maybe Jenny is getting dressed.* So she went to look in the bathroom. But Jenny was not there either.

Mrs. Jensen quickly went all through the house looking for little Jenny. But Jenny was not anywhere. She was missing!

Jenny's mother was becoming very scared. Then she looked out the kitchen window. In the deep snow she saw tiny footprints and little wagon wheel tracks leading away from the house.

Quickly, Mrs. Jensen put on her heavy coat and snow boots. Then she went out the back door and began following the footprints in the snow.

The footprints led her to the front sidewalk. Then they went down the block. And they went around the corner and down to the second block. Then the third block! *Where did Jenny go?* thought Mrs. Jensen as she hurried along.

At last Jenny's tracks led up to the front door of their minister's house. And there on the porch was little Jenny and her wagon. "Mr. John," as the children called the minister, was on the porch smiling and talking to Jenny.

Mrs. Jensen was so scared, she ran up to the porch and began to scold Jenny. But Mr. John said, "Mrs. Jensen, wait just a minute.

I think you will understand why Jenny came to see me if you will look in her wagon."

In the wagon were two red bricks. Mrs. Jensen looked at Mr. John and down at Jenny. Then she said, "Jenny, honey, tell me about the bricks."

"Well, Mommy, Mr. John said at the meeting that we don't have enough money to build a bigger church. I wanted to help more people learn about Jesus. So I brought these two bricks from our garage to Mr. John to start building the new church."

"But two bricks are not enough to build a whole church, honey."

"I know, but if everybody brought two bricks, we might have enough for a whole wall."

Bending down, Mrs. Jensen gave Jenny a big hug. "You're right, honey. I should have thought of that myself. Let's leave the bricks here with Mr. John. Maybe he can think of what to do next."

"Don't worry, Jenny," said Mr. John. "I'll take the bricks to church tomorrow."

The next morning was Sunday. When Mr. John got up to speak at the church, he held up the two bricks that Jenny had brought. He told the whole church what she had done. Soon people were standing up to tell what *they* could do to help with the new church building.

"I can bring some lumber," said Mr. Peters.

"And I can bring the nails," said Mr. Dobbs.

"I have lots of tools that we can use," said Mr. Sanders.

"The children and I can help carry things for you," said Mrs. Jenkins, the first-grade Sunday school teacher.

"And I can make sandwiches and cookies for everybody who is working," laughed Grandma Wipple.

Before long, they had solved

their problem. The new church was going to be built after all.

After church that day, Jenny got lots of hugs from everyone in the church. It was a wonderful day!

"A little child showed them the way to go."
—Isaiah 11:6

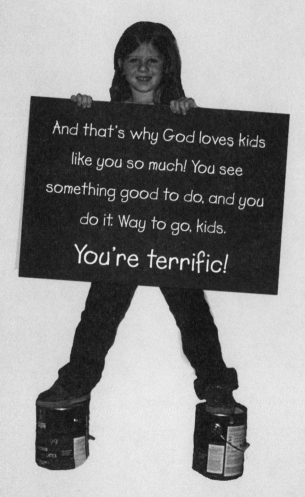

And that's why God loves kids like you so much! You see something good to do, and you do it. Way to go, kids.

You're terrific!

You Are You—
2
and Nobody Else

"God even knows ....

how many hairs are on your head." Matthew 10:30 ......

One of a Kind

One of a kind is all you'll find—
There'll never be even two—
For one of a kind,
    you're sure to find,
Is all God made of you!
You're different from
    your mom and dad,
Your sisters and your brothers.
So celebrate the special you—
Unique among the others!

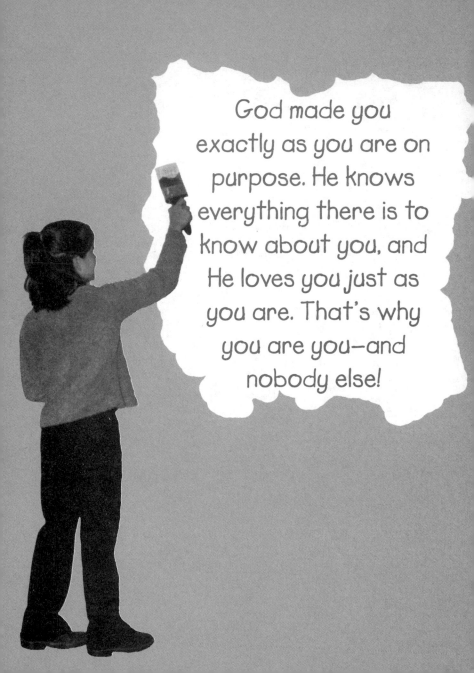

The Slowest Rider

Jeremy was a born loser. He often said he was just like Charlie Brown in the *Peanuts* cartoon strip. He lost at everything he tried. He lost at baseball and soccer and football. He lost at spelling and math and science. He even lost at lunch, because he never had anything to trade that anybody else wanted. He was a loser. That's all there was to it.

Jeremy's schoolteacher, Miss Mitchell, noticed that he had a hard time making friends and being part of the group. After all, nobody wanted a loser on their team. And nobody wanted a loser as a friend. So Jeremy spent most of his time alone.

One Saturday Miss Mitchell walked the few blocks from her home to the market. She had some shopping to do. She bought milk, bread, fruit, and a Snicker's bar, her favorite treat. After she paid the cashier at the market, she took her sack of groceries and started walking back home.

About a block from her house, Miss Mitchell heard someone calling her name.

"Hi, Miss Mitchell!"

When she turned around, she saw Jeremy coming up behind her on his bicycle.

"Hi, Jeremy!" she called back.

Jeremy rode up beside Miss Mitchell and slowed down. Miss Mitchell kept walking as they talked about school and sports. And Jeremy rode his bike alongside her very slowly.

Miss Mitchell noticed that Jeremy had great balance on his bike, even when he rode very slowly. So she began to walk even more slowly to see what he would do.

It didn't matter

how slowly Miss Mitchell walked, Jeremy could ride his bike and stay balanced. He was the best slow rider she had ever seen.

"Jeremy, you really ride your bike well," said Miss Mitchell.

"Thanks," said Jeremy shyly.

"How do you stay balanced when you're riding so slowly?"

"I don't know; it's just easy for me. I've always been able to do it."

Miss Mitchell smiled to herself. She knew what she was going to do Monday at school.

At recess on Monday, Miss Mitchell announced that they were going to have a contest—a very special bike riding contest. "The reason this contest is so special is because it's a *slow* bike riding contest."

"A *slow* riding contest?" asked Philip. "What's that mean?"

"The person who can ride a bike the slowest for the longest without falling over will win the contest," said Miss Mitchell, glancing up at Jeremy. He was grinning from ear to ear.

"All right, everyone, line up with your bikes at this line." Philip, Andy, and James all lined up together. Two or three other kids lined up in the middle. And Jeremy slowly came up to the line at the far end.

"Now, when I say go, get on your bikes and ride them toward the baseball field as slowly as you can without falling over. Ready? Set. Go!"

Two of the kids had hardly begun before they had lost their balance and were out of the race. James tried to be clever and ride without any hands, but he found out he couldn't do it and go slowly. So he was out. Philip just couldn't ride slowly, no matter how hard he tried. He finally gave up.

Finally, only Andy and Jeremy were left. And Andy was having to work really hard to keep his balance while Jeremy was just slowly riding toward the baseball field. It seemed easy for him.

"Wow, Miss Mitchell!" said Philip, now

watching Jeremy with new admiration. "How does he do that?"

"He's just very talented, Philip," she smiled. "Haven't you ever noticed?"

"No, ma'am, I guess I haven't."

"Auugh!" yelled Andy as he finally lost his balance and toppled over.

Jeremy slowly rode on toward the base-ball field. *I won! I won!* he thought.

Miss Mitchell called all the kids together on the playground. "Boys and girls, I am proud to award this first-place cap to Jeremy Johnson, the first and very best slow bike rider at Travis Elementary School."

"Hooray for Jeremy!"

yelled one of the little girls who thought Jeremy was nice.

Then all the kids joined in. "Way to go, Jeremy!" "Attaboy, Jeremy!" "Great job, Jeremy!"

Miss Mitchell slowly backed out of the circle of children and watched Jeremy receive his deserved praise. Now *she* was the one grinning.

After school that day, Miss Mitchell was in her classroom grading papers when she heard a knock on the door. She looked up to see Jeremy.

"May I come in, Miss Mitchell?" he asked quietly.

"Sure, Jeremy. What can I do for you?"

"You already did it, Miss Mitchell. Thanks for letting me win that contest today."

"Now, wait just a minute, Jeremy. I did not *let* you win. You won that contest fair and square."

"Well, I guess so, but you picked a contest you knew I could win."

"All I did was give you a chance to show your friends the special talent that God gave you, Jeremy. Every person has some gifts from God, and He gave you a couple of really good ones."

About that time, Philip and James stuck their heads in the room, and Philip said, "Hey, Jeremy, we're going swimming down at the park. Want to go with us?"

"Sure!" smiled Jeremy with surprise. "I'll be right there." Then, turning back to Miss Mitchell, and making sure the other boys weren't watching, he kissed her on the cheek. "Anyway, thanks for what you did."

"You're welcome, Jeremy. Say, what else do you do really well?"

With a great big grin, Jeremy took off his "Best Slow Bike Rider" cap, took a big bow, and laughed as he ran out of the room, "Slow swimming!"

God made you exactly as you are for a very special purpose, and He loves you just as you are.

That's why you are you... and nobody else!

"We all have different gifts from God. And we should use our gifts to help other people."
—Romans 12:6

You Are Smart

3

Wise and Smart

It's very smart and very wise

To look at things with heaven's eyes,

To do the things God wants you to,

To be a friend who's good and true,

To show God's kindness day by day,

To teach His love by what you say.

It's very wise and very smart

To share God's grace with all your heart.

And knowledge will be pleasing to you." Proverbs 2:10

Kids are smart!
Sometimes, and in
some ways, you are
even smarter than
adults. That's because
God made you
that way.

Flowers That Live Forever

As Julie walked home from school on Tuesday, she noticed something odd at the house on the corner. Usually Miss Margie was outside working in her pretty flower garden and Miss Bonnie was sitting in the swing on the porch reading her book. The two older ladies had been best friends all their lives. Now they were housemates and took care of each other.

But today they weren't there. Julie saw that a round wreath of flowers was hanging on the front door and several cars were parked along the street. *They must be having a party*, she thought. So she went home without stopping for cookies and lemonade as she usually did.

That night Julie's mom came to Julie's room. She said that Miss Margie would not be working in her flowers anymore when Julie came home from school. She had gone to be with God. And Miss Bonnie was very sad. She said it might be best for Julie not to stop after school for a few days until Miss Bonnie felt better.

Every day, Julie watched to see if Miss Bonnie was in the swing on the porch. But she never was. After about a week, Julie went up and knocked on the door. Miss Bonnie came to the door. She looked as if she had been crying.

"What do you want?" she said gruffly.

Frightened, Julie said, "I just wanted to say I'm sorry Miss Margie had to go away."

"Well, she's gone, and that's that," Miss Bonnie said angrily. "So there's no need for you to come around here any-more." Then she slammed the door.

37

Julie was hurt by Miss Bonnie's mean words. She turned and walked sadly off the porch and down the block to her house.

As time went by, Julie noticed that weeds began to grow up in Miss Margie's flower garden. The lawn needed mowing too. She also saw that the front porch was covered with leaves and the swing needed painting. The whole house looked so sad, just like Miss Bonnie.

That afternoon, on her way home from school, Julie decided to help. So she stopped and pulled a few weeds out of the flowers. Then she went home. And every day after school, she pulled a few more weeds, getting closer and closer to the front porch as she worked.

Then one day, as she was pulling weeds around the bottom step of the porch, the front door burst open, and Miss Bonnie came storming out onto the porch.

"What do you think you're doing, you little do-gooder?"

"Miss Margie would be sad to see her flowers dying," said Julie bravely. "If we keep them alive, it will be like having Miss Margie here too."

"I told you Miss Margie's gone. She's not coming back. Now you get out of here, and don't come back!" Then she went back in the house and slammed the door again.

The next day, Julie decided to try a different idea. She wrote a note and stuck it in her Bible at John 11:25–26. On her way to school, she put her Bible with the note and a little bag of homemade cookies into Miss Bonnie's mailbox. Here's what the note said:

Dear Miss Bonnie,

Miss Margie's not really dead, you know. Please read the verse I marked in my Bible. I hope you like the cookies.

Love,
Julie

That afternoon, as she came to the house on the corner, Julie saw Miss Bonnie sitting in the swing on her porch. She had Julie's Bible in her lap.

"Hello, Miss Bonnie," said Julie shyly.

"Hello, Julie dear," said Miss Bonnie with a little smile. "Would you like a cookie and some lemonade?"

"Uh, I guess so," said Julie. And she came slowly up onto the porch. She was still a little afraid of what Miss Bonnie might do.

"I've been reading the Scripture you marked. I've read it over and over and over again. In fact, I've read it so many times, I have it memorized: 'I am the resurrection and the life. He who believes in me will have life even if he dies. And he who lives and believes in me will never die.' Thank you for showing it to me. It helped me a lot."

"You're welcome, Miss Bonnie. I know Miss Margie would not want you to be sad about her being with God."

"You know, Julie, you're absolutely right. She wouldn't. You're a very smart girl. So I think it's time I got busy around here and fixed this old place up. Would you like to help?"

"I sure would!" said Julie. "Where should we start?"

"I think we should pull the rest of those weeds out of Miss Margie's flowers. Then we'll sweep the porch and mow the lawn."

"And paint the swing?"

"Yes," Miss Bonnie laughed, "and paint the swing."

"I'll bet Miss Margie's smiling down at us now, Miss Bonnie."

"Yes, child," she said glancing up at the blue sky, "I'll just bet she is too."

"I sure do miss her, don't you?"

"Yes, dear, I surely

do miss her. But having you here helps. You remind me so much of her. Come on, let's get started!"

"That's what life's all about—laughing and loving each other, and knowing they're not really gone when they die."
—Charles Ingalls,
Little House on the Prairie

Sometimes kids are clever and wise. You help others see things with heaven's eyes.

You're so smart!

Inside Your Heart

Inside your heart
There is a part—
A very, very special part—
That you should dare
To gladly share,
The part that shows
You really care.

"Care for one another." 1 Corinthians 12:25

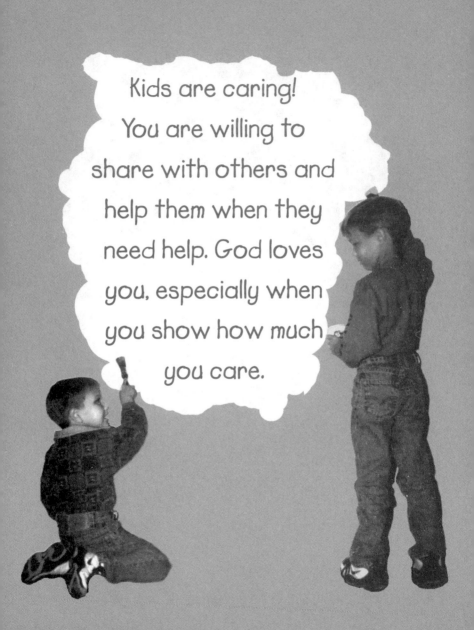

Kids are caring!
You are willing to
share with others and
help them when they
need help. God loves
you, especially when
you show how much
you care.

Popping a Wheelie

Finally the big day had come! Mark was so excited that he could hardly finish eating his breakfast. He wanted to get going.

For many months, Mark had been look-ing at a beautiful ten-speed Red Flyer in Parker's Bicycle Shop downtown. He had always wanted a bike like that. Besides, his old blue bike was falling apart. The fenders were rusted, and the paint was chipped off. The grips on the handlebars were cracked and broken. And the chain kept coming off. He really needed a new bike.

Most of his friends had new ten-speeds. Their parents had given them the bikes. But Mark's dad had died when Mark was just a little guy, and his mom had to work hard just to pay their rent and buy food.

There was no way she could buy Mark a bicycle. So Mark had decided to earn the money himself to buy the Red Flyer.

All spring and summer, Mark had been working a newspaper route. He got up every morning at five o'clock to roll his papers and get them ready. Then he loaded the papers in his bicycle basket and rode his route, throwing the papers on the porches of his customers. It was hard getting up that early every day, but Mark was willing to do it. He really wanted that new bike before school started.

He had also done odd jobs around his neighborhood to earn extra money. He raked leaves for Mr. Thompson. He painted Miss Williams's new fence. He mowed his grandparents' lawn. And he took care of the Stevenses' dog, Rusty, while they were gone on vacation. All in all, Mark had saved up eighty-nine dollars.

That was exactly how much the Red Flyer cost. And today was the day he was going down to get it.

After breakfast, Mark hugged his mother and ran out the door. He jumped onto his old blue bike and rode toward town. He could feel the eighty-nine dollars in his jeans' pocket. And he was so excited!

Just think! On the way home I'll be riding my brand-new Red Flyer, he thought to himself.

"Yippeee!" he yelled and popped a wheelie on Old Blue to celebrate.

When he got to town, he parked in front of the bicycle shop and pushed down the kickstand. As he ran up the front steps, he heard someone say, "Hi, Mark!"

He looked to his right and saw his friend Tracey leaning on her crutches in front of the store window next-door to the bicycle shop.

"Oh hi, Trace! How ya doin'?" He glanced longingly at the bicycle shop and then walked over to say hello.

"I'm great, thanks. What's up?"

Mark showed Tracey the Red Flyer and talked about how excited he was to be getting it.

"Wow! That's great, Mark! I'd really like to have some new wheels too. Want to see them?"

"Sure. Where are they?"

Tracey turned around and led Mark back to the other shop. Then Mark saw Tracey's eyes light up. In the window of Stiger's Drug Store was a shiny, silver, child-sized wheelchair.

"It's perfect for me, Mark! Look how small it is. It would be so great to have one of these. My arms get so sore and tired using these crutches all the time."

"Well, how long will you have to use the crutches?"

"The doctor says I'll probably need them

from now on. My leg was hurt too badly in the accident to ever be right again."

"Oh. Well, can't your dad get the wheel-chair for you?"

"No. With all the doctor bills and stuff, there's just no more money. Maybe some-day, though. I'd like to earn the money myself, like you did, but with these crutch-es, there's not much I can do. Meanwhile," she smiled, "I can dream, can't I?"

"Sure, Trace. Sure you can," said Mark quietly.

"Well, see you later, Mark. I've got to go home and get supper for Dad. Since Mom

died in the accident, I have to help all I can."

"Yeah, Trace, see you at school Monday."

Tracey took one more long look at the little wheelchair and then bumped away down the sidewalk on her crutches. Mark stood for a long time watching her go. Then he turned and started into the bicycle shop.

Just as he put his hand on the shop door handle, he stopped. Then a big smile lit up his face. He glanced back at the Red Flyer in the window and shrugged his shoulders. "Oh well," he said out loud to the bike. "You'll still be here in six months." Then he patted Old Blue's torn seat and walked into the shop next-door.

"Hey, Mr. Stiger. How much is this little wheelchair?"

"It's eighty-three dollars, plus tax, Mark."

"How much is the tax?"

"Well, let's see. It's five dollars and ten cents."

Mark quietly pulled the eighty-nine dollars he had saved for his new bike out of his pocket and put it on the counter.

"Could you please deliver that wheelchair to Tracey Martin's house? And don't tell her who sent it, okay?"

"Sure, Mark, if you're sure that's what you want to do."

"Yeah, I'm sure, Mr. Stiger."

Mark took his ninety cents change and left. On his way home, he stopped at the hardware store and used the ninety cents to buy a small can of bright red paint. He would have a new red bike after all, and Tracey would have new wheels too. It had been a wonderful day!

The next morning, Mark went to the garage to get his bike to run his paper route. There in the drive-

way sat the beautiful Red Flyer he wanted so badly. A note was tied to the handlebars. He opened it and slowly began to smile.

Dear Mark,

Mr. Stiger told me what a nice thing you did today for little Tracey. So I'd like to do something nice for you. Here's that Red Flyer you've been working so hard to buy. You can pay me for it a little each week from your paper route. Hope you like it.

Mr. Parker
Parker's Bike Shop

"Yipeee!" shouted Mark. Then he loaded his papers in the basket, jumped on his new Red Flyer, and popped a wheelie going out of the driveway.

"God cares for you."

—1 Peter 5:7

That's how it works, kids.
When you show how much you
care, it helps other people
remember to care too.

Thanks for caring!

"Love each other deeply with all your heart."

1 Peter 1:22

Jesus Loves Me

Jesus loves me: this I know,

For the Bible tells me so.

Little ones to Him belong;

They are weak, but He is strong.

Yes, Jesus loves me!

Yes, Jesus loves me!

Yes, Jesus loves me!

The Bible tells me so.

—Anna B. Warner, 1860

The Bestest Birthday Ever

J. T. was so excited that he could hardly go to sleep. Tomorrow was his big birthday party! His grandmother had promised him that he could have all his favorites. Everything would be chocolate: chocolate cake, chocolate ice cream, and even fudge topping.

All his friends were coming too. And J. T. just knew he would get the toy he wanted so badly—a Transmorgifier! He had been begging for it for weeks. Surely tomorrow someone would give it to him. He thought it would be the best birthday ever.

All his pals from school were coming over—Donny, James, Jeff, and Tip. Oh yeah, and little Grant was coming too. *Little Grant!* J. T. sat straight up in bed. *Oh no!* he thought. *That will never work.*

Grant was J. T.'s younger cousin, who followed J. T. around like a shadow. He thought J. T. was the coolest dude in the world. And he hung on J. T.'s every word. J. T. liked Grant too. He was a neat little kid.

But there was a big problem. Grant was really allergic to chocolate. It made him very sick. If he ate chocolate, his eyes would swell shut, and he couldn't breathe.

J. T. thought and thought about the problem. What could he do? He *really* wanted to have chocolate cake and ice cream at his party. After all, it was *his* birthday. He should get to have *his* favorite, and *his* favorite was chocolate. But if he did, little Grant would not have any fun at all.

Finally, J. T. crawled out of bed and went over to his desk. He turned on the desk lamp and got out a piece of paper and a pencil. He wrote a note to his grandmother. Then he folded it up and went down the hall to her room. He slipped the note under her door and went back to his room.

The next day at two o'clock, all J. T.'s friends came to the house for the party. Little Grant came too. There were colorful streamers hung in the living room. Music was playing, and Grandmother had lots of fun games planned. Best of all, there was cake and ice cream for later.

After a few games, J. T. got to open his presents. He got some really fun gifts, but each time he opened a box, he secretly hoped it was the Transmorgifier he wanted so badly. He was really disappointed when the gift he wanted the most was not there. Still, he smiled and thanked everybody for the nice things he got.

Then it was time for the food. Grandmother came into the room carrying a huge cake covered with burning candles. Everyone sang "Happy Birthday," and J. T. blew out the ten candles with one big breath. The guys all cheered and gathered around as Grandmother began to cut the cake.

Grant's eyes lit up when he saw that it was a huge white cake with sugary white icing and vanilla ice cream with whipped cream. J. T. grinned happily as he watched his little cousin lick the last drop of ice cream from his spoon and eat the cake crumbs off his tiny fingers.

At last the party was over, and all J. T.'s buddies left. Grant came over to J. T. and threw his chubby little arms around his neck. He gave J. T. a big, sticky kiss and said, "Thanks, J. T. Nobody ever has cake I can eat at parties. This was the bestest birthday party ever!"

Then, wiggling down from J. T.'s arms, he ran out the door toward his mom's van, yelling, "Wait! I'll be right back. I forgot something!"

In about two minutes, Grant came running back and handed J. T. a big present. "I forgot to give you your present. Hope you like it!" And he dashed away again to the van.

After Grant left, J. T. was thinking about how great it was to see Grant eating the white cake and ice cream. It hadn't been so bad giving up his favorite chocolate for his sweet little cousin after all. As he thought about Grant and the party, he was opening Grant's present. And there it was— the Transmorgifier!

J. T. yelped with joy! Then he turned to

75

his grandma, who was smiling as she watched, and he said, "Grandma, I think Grant was right. This was the bestest birthday party ever."

"God loved the world so much that he gave his only Son...so that whoever believes in him may not be lost, but have eternal life."

—John 3:16

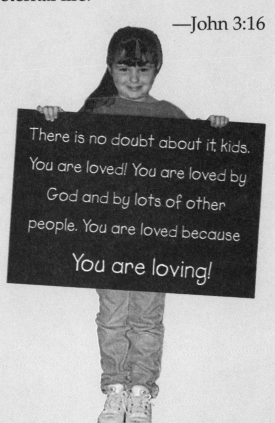

There is no doubt about it, kids. You are loved! You are loved by God and by lots of other people. You are loved because

You are loving!

You Are Giving

6

Listen, Little Child

Little child,

Meek and mild,

Listen to God's wind:

"Take your cup

And fill it up;

Then share it with a friend."

Little child,

Meek and mild,

Listen to God's words:

"Take a shred

Of your sweet bread

And feed the little birds."

—M. H., *Into My Heart*

"God loves a cheerful giver." 2 Corinthians 9:7

Wow, kids! You are so exciting! It's great to see how you can get people to work together to help others by giving their best.

Giving Your Best Is Best

It was the dog's picture on the front page of the newspaper that ten-year-old Becky saw first. The big German shepherd police dog had been shot and killed in the line of duty. Looking at the picture made Becky remember her own dog, Jeepers. They had had to put Jeepers to sleep a few weeks before when he had been hit by a car. And she began to cry as she read.

The story told how the police dog, Samson, had attacked a criminal who was trying to shoot his policeman partner. The criminal shot twice, once at the policeman and once at Samson. The policeman had been protected by a bulletproof vest. But Samson was killed.

"Mom," she said, "why can't dogs have bulletproof vests too?"

"I don't know, honey. Is there such a thing as a bulletproof vest for dogs?"

The idea perked Becky up a bit. "I don't know. How could I find out, Mom?"

"Well, let's see," said her mom, thinking out loud. "Maybe you could call Uncle Pete and ask him. Since he's a policeman, he might know."

"Can I call him right now?"

"Sure, I suppose so."

Becky dialed her favorite uncle's phone number at home and waited while the phone rang twice. Then she heard her uncle's big, happy voice.

"Hello."

"Uncle Pete, this is Becky."

"Well, hello, pumpkin!" he laughed. "What's up?"

By talking to Uncle Pete, Becky learned that one company did make bulletproof vests for police dogs. The company was in Chicago, Illinois.

"But," he said, "I think the vests cost a lot of money. And we have eight police dogs."

Becky's mom called the Chicago telephone information operator and got the number of the company. Then they called the company. They found out that each dog vest cost about five hundred dollars.

"Wow!" sighed Becky. "That's a lot of money."

"It sure is," said her mom. "Well, let's think about it."

Later that week, Becky said, "Mom, I've been thinking about those poor dogs with no vests. And I want to do something to help. All right?"

"Yes, it's all right with me. What do you want to do?"

"I want to talk to people and see if I can raise enough money to buy vests for our police dogs."

"Well, that's a great thing to want to do, honey. Do you realize you're talking about—"

"I know, I know, four thousand dollars. But if everybody will help, we can do it."

"Okay, Becky, if that's what you really want to do, I'll help too. How would you like to talk to my civic club about it on Monday?"

"Sure! Thanks, Mom!"

Becky and her mom got busy making posters about

the drive to buy dog vests. Then they addressed envelopes for people to use to send in donations. Next Becky started calling people, asking for donations and setting up times to talk to clubs and groups all over town. She talked to her friends and teachers at school and at church too. Some of her friends began helping Becky raise the money. Uncle Pete helped too.

After several weeks and a lot of hard work, Becky's mom said one night, "Becky, I think we should see how much more money we need to raise." So they sat down at their dining room table and counted all the money that had been donated. When they finished counting, they had $3,985.

"Wow, Mom! We only need fifteen more dollars!"

"That's right. And I think I know where to get it."

"Really? Where?"

"Do you remember the money we were saving to buy Jeepers a new doghouse?"

"Yes."

"Well, don't you think Jeepers would want to help his doggy friends, too, if he were here?"

"He sure would! How much money do we have?"

Becky's mom went to the cabinet and took down a dog food can. She took off the plastic lid and took out some dollar bills. Becky counted the money and discovered they had twelve dollars.

"Only three more dollars…" said Becky. "I know! My piggy bank!"

She ran to her room and came back with the pink piggy bank. She emptied it on the table and began counting. "…two ninety-seven, two ninety-eight, two ninety-nine, three dollars! Yippee!" she cheered. "We made it! We made it!"

The next day, Becky and her mom drove to police headquarters. They went in and asked to see the chief of police. Uncle Pete went with them. Then they gave the chief the four thousand dollars they had raised for the police dogs' bulletproof vests.

The chief smiled a huge smile and thanked them. Then he called Uncle Pete aside and gave him some instructions. Uncle Pete grinned and left, saying, "I'll be right back, Becky. Wait here."

While Uncle Pete was gone, a newspaper man came in looking for a story and found out what Becky had done. He asked her some questions about the money she had raised and asked if he could take her picture for the paper.

Just as he was ready to take the picture, Uncle Pete came back. But he was not alone. Eight excited police dogs greeted Becky with wagging tails and wet, sloppy kisses. It was as if they knew what a wonderful thing she had done for them.

The next Friday at the annual policemen's banquet, Becky was the guest of honor. She received her own special police uniform. And the chief of police swore her in as a junior canine officer. They also gave her a tiny German shepherd puppy named Buddy to be her very own police dog. And you guessed it—he was wearing a tiny bulletproof vest!

Now, that was a great picture, and it showed up on the front page of the next day's paper.

"Give, and you will receive.... You will be given so much that it will spill into your lap. The way you give to others is the way God will give to you."

—Luke 6:38

God loves it when you give to others. That's because your giving reminds others to give too.

Thanks for giving so much!

You Are Kind

7

Hugs of Kindness

Acts of kindness and of love

Are just like hugs from up above.

So put your arms around your friend

And hug until the heartaches mend.

For there is nothing quite so kind

As hugs from heaven to mankind.

"Be kind to one another." Ephesians 4:32

Head to Head

Austin sat holding his head in his hands and stared at the dirt in the dugout. The baseball game was going okay. The Eagles were winning. He had even hit a home run during the last inning. He should be happy. But he wasn't. Playing ball just wasn't as much fun without his best friend, Rusty.

For several days, Rusty had not been able to play baseball. He had been in the hospital. Austin's mom told him that Rusty had cancer. He was having to take special medicine, and the doctors were giving him some stuff called "chemo" to make him better.

Austin's mom had taken him to the hospital to see Rusty one day. Rusty was laughing and talking like normal, but Austin thought he looked kind of strange. He had plastic tubes in his arms, and there were blinking and beeping machines all around his bed. It was pretty scary.

Rusty acted brave. He said he would be home pretty soon and would be back playing ball before the big game with the Giants next week. Austin hoped he was right. It was boring without Rusty around.

A few days later, Austin was at the baseball field again. Today they were playing the Bulldogs from across town. The Bulldogs were a good team, so he would really have to play well. But he was having a hard time getting excited. Rusty still wasn't there.

"Hey, Austin!"

Austin looked around. It was Rusty! He was running across the infield waving at Austin. And he was all suited up, ready to play.

"Hey, Rusty! Boy am I glad to see you!"

"Yeah, me too. I finally got out of the hospital yesterday."

Austin noticed that Rusty was wearing a bright green baseball cap that came down low over his eyes and ears.

"Hey, Rusty, neat cap. Can I see it?" Austin asked, reaching for the cap.

"No, man. Uh, don't take the cap, okay?" Rusty said, pulling away from Austin.

"Well, okay, Rus. I just wanted to look at it."

"Maybe later. Okay, Aus?"

"Sure, Rus. Sure."

"Come on, Aus, let's throw some balls around and get loosened up for the game."

Pretty soon, the game began. Austin, Rusty, and all the Eagles played hard, but so did the Bulldogs. By the end of the eighth inning, the score was tied four to four. The coach gave them a pep talk before the ninth inning, and they went out to take the field.

The Bulldogs scored two runs in the top of the ninth inning. Then it was the Eagles' turn to bat. The first batter hit a single and got on first. Then it was Austin's turn to bat. He hit a line drive to left field. The runner on first went to second, and Austin ran to first. They had two on base and no outs.

The third batter struck out. Then the fourth batter hit a pop-up fly, and the shortstop caught it. Now they had two on base and two outs. The next batter up was Rusty. He banged the bat against his shoes, pulled his cap down hard, and swung the bat up onto his shoulder.

The first pitch was right across the plate, and Rusty hit it hard. It went right over the second baseman's head and sailed between the fielders to the back fence. The player on second and Austin headed for home. Rusty was running as hard as he could...around first...around second...around third. And then, the ball came flying into home plate just as Rusty got there. He hit the dirt and slid into home, hands and face first. He was safe! He had won the game for them.

But when Rusty got up and began dusting himself off, everyone stopped cheering and just stared. His green cap had fallen off when he slid into home plate. Rusty was bald! His hair was completely gone.

Rusty quickly grabbed the cap and shoved it back onto his bald head, but it was too late. Some of the Bulldogs were laughing. And Rusty's face turned red because he was embarrassed.

Then he ran off the field to where his dad was standing, and they quickly left the ball-park.

Austin just stood there staring after Rusty. Bald! He just couldn't believe it.

"Austin! Over here!"

Austin finally looked around and noticed their coach was motioning for him. Austin trotted over to where the Eagles were gathered around the coach. Then the coach explained that Rusty's hair had come out because of that "chemo" stuff he had to take in the hospital. He said that his hair might come back in later but Rusty was pretty embarrassed about it right now. So the team needed to be kind about it.

Suddenly, Austin got a big smile on his

face. When the coach left, Austin said, "Hey, fellas, huddle up. I've got an idea."

All the guys gathered around Austin, and he explained his idea to them.

"Yeah! Great idea, Austin! Let's do it!"

"Okay, guys, we'll do it at the Giants game on Thursday," said Austin. "And I'll go first."

"Right! See you Thursday."

Two days later, on Thursday, the big game with the Giants was getting ready to start. All the Eagles were huddled together near their dugout, except for Rusty. He hadn't come yet.

"Hey, look! Here comes Rusty!" said Joey.

Austin stepped out of the group and went out to meet Rusty.

"Hey, Rus!" shouted Austin, running toward him.

"Hey, Aus," said Rusty quietly, keeping his head down.

"Man, I'm glad you made it!" said Austin.

"Well, I couldn't let the team down...no matter what."

"Yeah, well, thanks, Rus." And as the rest of the team came over to them, Austin said, "We didn't want to let you down either."

Rusty glanced up and said, "What do you mean?"

"This!" said Austin, taking off his own

cap to reveal a shaved head. "If it's good enough for you, Rus, it's good enough for me."

"And us!" laughed the rest of the team, taking off their caps to show their shaved heads.

"Yeah," laughed Joey, "we decided we would be the bald Eagles!"

"Oh, man," said Rusty with his eyes wide open and starting to mist. "I can't believe you guys did this. Thanks."

"It's okay, Rus. We're a team. You'd have done it for us," said Austin.

"Right!" said Joey. "Enough of this

mushy stuff. Now let's get out there and win!"

With a whoop and a cheer, the bald Eagles took the field. And they played the best game of the year, beating the Giants ten–zip.

"Do for other people what you want them to do for you."

—Luke 6:31

The Bible verse above is all about kindness. It's called the Golden Rule, and it's what God wants us to do for each other. Thanks for showing us how to be kind, kids.

Thanks for being so kind!

Your Very Own Story

8

Your Story

There are stories, new and old;

There are stories, strange and bold;

There are stories full of fun

And tales of heroes on the run.

There are stories full of mystery

And stories based on ancient history.

But there's no story, fake or true,

As terrific as the tale of you!

"Always be ready to answer everyone who asks

you to explain about the hope you have." 1 Peter 3:15

Always be ready to tell your story! People want to know all about you. They want to know why you believe what you do and why you do what you do.

Draw your picture here.

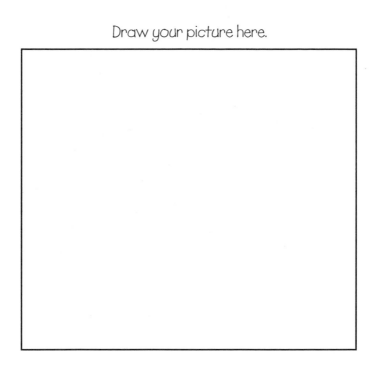

Your Very Own Story

Here's your chance to practice telling your very own story about a time when you were kind or caring or loving, just like Jesus. Write it on these next few pages. And have fun doing it.

Your Very Own Story

_____

_____

_____

_____

_____

_____

_____

_____

_____

_____

_____

_____

_____

_____

Your Very Own Story

_____

_____

_____

_____

_____

_____

_____

_____

_____

_____

_____

_____

_____

_____

_____

_____

Your Very Own Story

Your Very Own Story

_____

_____

_____

_____

_____

_____

_____

_____

_____

_____

_____

_____

_____

_____

_____

"Tell me the old, old story

Of Jesus and his love,"

And you will tell me

Your own story—

And that's the very best story of all.